P9-DNK-764

Jeanie & Genie

FOLLOW YOUR ART

 BY **TRISH GRANTED**
ILLUSTRATED BY **MANUELA LÓPEZ**

LITTLE SIMON
New York   London   Toronto   Sydney   New Delhi

 **LITTLE SIMON**

An imprint of Simon & Schuster Children's Publishing Division · 1230 Avenue of the Americas, New York, New York 10020 · First Little Simon paperback edition January 2021
Copyright © 2021 by Simon & Schuster, Inc.
All rights reserved, including the right of reproduction in whole or in part in any form.
LITTLE SIMON is a registered trademark of Simon & Schuster, Inc., and associated colophon is a trademark of Simon & Schuster, Inc.
For information about special discounts for bulk purchases, please contact Simon & Schuster Special Sales at 1-866-506-1949 or business@simonandschuster.com.
The Simon & Schuster Speakers Bureau can bring authors to your live event. For more information or to book an event contact the Simon & Schuster Speakers Bureau at 1-866-248-3049 or visit our website at www.simonspeakers.com.
Designed by Brittany Fetcho.
Manufactured in the United States of America 1120 MTN
10 9 8 7 6 5 4 3 2 1
Cataloging-in-Publication Data is available for this title from the Library of Congress.
ISBN 978-1-5344-7472-7 (hc)
ISBN 978-1-5344-7471-0 (pbk)
ISBN 978-1-5344-7473-4 (eBook)

TABLE OF CONTENTS

Chapter 1

A HAPPY ACCIDENT

Jeanie Bell was camped out under her favorite oak tree with her best friend, Willow Davis. It was recess at Rivertown Elementary, and the girls were each doing what they loved. Willow was practicing her cartwheels. And Jeanie was getting a head start on her homework.

Jeanie knew things were going to get *very* busy *very* soon. This week, classroom 2B had a field trip to the art museum, the school art fair, AND a big art project due!

"Ta-da!" Willow said as she finished a triple cartwheel.

Jeanie clapped for her friend. "My legs could use a stretch. Want to walk around the playground?"

"Sure!" said Willow. "But I'm going to *cartwheel* around the playground."

Jeanie laughed. As she walked— and Willow cartwheeled—Jeanie looked at what her classmates were doing. Some were swinging on the swings. Others were playing with a deck of cards. Some had soccer balls and footballs and Frisbees. And one classmate, a boy named Leo Gomez, was doing some sort of art project. As Jeanie walked closer, she didn't notice that Willow was also cartwheeling closer, with no idea where she was going. She bumped right into Leo, and paint sprayed everywhere.

"Sorry!" cried Willow.

"That's okay," said Leo. "This piece is abstract. Accidents make it more . . . spontaneous. That's why I call them happy accidents!"

Jeanie looked around, impressed.

Leo had set up the playground merry-go-round as an outdoor easel. A large piece of paper was taped to it. As the merry-go-round spun, the paint Leo squirted onto the paper made amazing swirls of color.

Leo took off the sheet of paper and laid it in the grass. He looked at it thoughtfully.

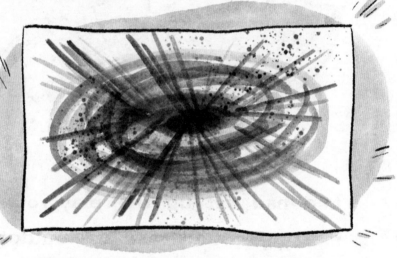

"What do you think?" he asked.

"I love the colors!" Willow exclaimed. "They're so bright and cheerful. I love to paint, but I've never done something like this!"

"Thanks," said Leo. "Did you make that bracelet you're wearing?"

"Yes!" Willow said. "Jeanie and I were beading the other day, and I made this flower charm bracelet because I *love* flowers."

"The art museum has some nice paintings of flowers," Leo told her. "You should check them out on our field trip tomorrow."

"It's so cool that we're doing projects inspired by the art we see," Willow said dreamily.

"*And* we're helping set up the art fair later in the week," Jeanie said. "Which means we won't have a lot of free time. I'd better get back to my homework."

The two friends waved at Leo and headed back to the oak tree. Jeanie really admired Leo's creativity. And Willow's, too. Even if Willow's creative accidents could get . . . complicated. Because Willow had a secret.

ART-SPIRATION

When Willow woke up the next morning, she could barely contain her excitement. She was going on her first ever field trip.

She wore her most artistic outfit to school: a pink striped top, gold sequin skirt, and a beret. She added layers of sparkly beaded necklaces. And her magic lamp charm, of course! Because Willow's secret? Her secret was that she was actually . . . a genie! A real-live genie who could grant wishes.

At ten o'clock Ms. Patel and the art teacher, Mr. Bloom, herded everyone onto the bus. Willow bounced in her seat all the way to the museum.

"Do you think they have balloon art?" she asked Jeanie. "How much do you think the artists spend on glitter and puffy paint? Will there be gum wrapper portraits of Cinderella and every single fairy tale princess *ever*?"

"Hmm, I'm not sure there's art like that," Jeanie told her. "It's more like pictures of fruit and landscapes."

"Oh, you mean cloudscapes? I love cloudscapes!" Willow exclaimed. She looked out the window and imagined the clouds transforming into all the magical things she loved most: shooting stars, ladybugs, and kittycorns with sequined horns.

When the class arrived at the museum, Willow and Jeanie found themselves next to Leo.

"I like your skirt!" Leo said. "Very Gustav Klimt."

Goose I've glimpsed? thought Willow. She was pretty sure geese were at the zoo, not the museum.

"Thanks . . . I think!" Willow said.

Mr. Bloom cleared his throat. "Class, follow me," he said. "First up are still lifes!"

In the gallery, Willow looked around at all the paintings of beautiful flowers. She spotted irises, tulips, and bright yellow sunflowers. But something was missing. . . .

No fuzzy pom-pom stickers! she thought. *How strange.* Willow always used those in her art. They were perfect for creating the furry centers of sunflowers. But Willow loved the paintings anyway.

Soon Mr. Bloom gathered everyone together. "I hope everyone is excited for the art fair, which opens on Friday evening!" he said. He explained that for the rest of the week they'd be working in small groups to curate a collection of their classmates' artwork. That meant they'd be going through artwork their classmates had made so far this year and choosing the best pieces to display at the art fair.

"Each group is going to choose artwork from a different category. Let's start with something wild—animal and nature scenes!" announced Mr. Bloom. He listed the students in that group before going on to abstract art—like the art Leo had been working on at the playground—and futuristic art, which meant paintings and drawings and sculptures that looked like they were from the future.

"Jeanie, Leo, and Willow," he said, "All three of you volunteered to set up our art fair, so thank you for that. Your group will be curating classroom 2B's still lifes! And don't forget—you will each be creating a new piece of artwork that can go into any category."

Willow bounced on her toes. She was so excited! She got to work with her best friend *and* Leo. Plus, they would be curating still lifes, just like the flower paintings she'd been admiring! She couldn't wait to get started.

Chapter 3

USE YOUR IMAGINATION

For the first time ever, Jeanie was running late.

It was Thursday morning, and she was supposed to meet Willow and Leo in the small gym to set up for the art fair. They had spent the whole week reviewing classroom 2B's still lifes and choosing which ones to display. Today they would add their own projects to the gallery.

For her project, Jeanie had decided to do a portrait of her dog, Bear, in the pointillist style of Seurat. Jeanie had spent hours capturing the many shades of Bear's yellow fur in dots of canary, lemon, and goldenrod.

"You've gone completely dotty!" Jake had told her.

When Jeanie got to the gym, she saw that dividers had been set up to make a small gallery for each category of art. Willow and Leo were inside, setting up their projects.

"Wow!" Jeanie said when she saw Willow's sculpture. It was a ballerina inspired by a Degas they'd seen at the museum. Willow's ballerina had a neon-pink tulle skirt and feathers in her hair.

"Very bold!" Leo said. "Let's put it on a pedestal."

"And I'll hang Bear on the far wall," Jeanie added. "Leo, where should we put yours?"

"I've made a mobile," he announced, lifting a tangle of wooden shapes and string from his bag. "It will look great in that corner."

Jeanie and Willow watched as
Leo carefully hung the mobile in
the air. The pieces floated and spun
gracefully. Jeanie couldn't take her
eyes off it.

"It's really cool, Leo," she said.
"But . . . what is it?"

Leo's face lit up. "If you look closely, you can see that the lowest pieces show the galloping motion of a horse's legs. And in the front, the wave of his mane billows as he charges forward. This piece is all about movement and energy!"

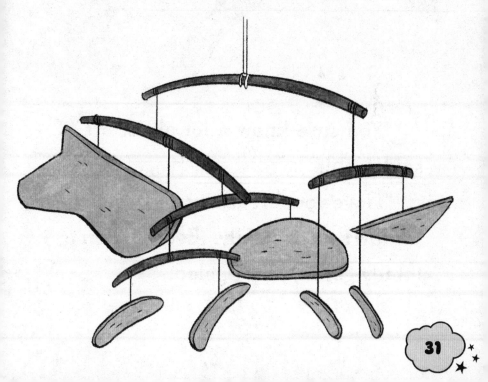

"You sure know a lot about art," said Jeanie.

"I love your creativity and vision," Willow said dreamily. "Even if I don't totally get it." She giggled.

Just then the Lee triplets passed by.

"Look! It's a giant wind chime!" they shouted.

Leo sighed. "Sometimes you need to use your imagination to see. Art can be magical!"

Jeanie caught Willow's eye. The two girls giggled. They might not know that much about art, but they sure knew a lot about magic.

Leo watched the Lee triplets walk away. "I just *wish* I could make art come alive for everyone," he said.

Jeanie's eyes went wide. Had Leo just said the *w* word?

Willow's magic lamp necklace began to glow.

Suddenly a golden flash lit up the room. . . .

Chapter 4

FUNNY FEELINGS

Willow froze. She knew what that golden flash meant—she'd just granted a wish!

She exchanged a nervous glance with Jeanie. Her best friend was the only person outside her family who knew Willow was a genie.

Jeanie scanned the gym. Everything *looked* normal. Nothing had fallen over. Their art projects seemed fine. And Leo was his usual self.

"Some people have no taste!" he huffed. "No creativity! No vision!" He bent down and shoved his stuff into his bag. "Let's just meet tomorrow morning to finish setting up, okay?" He threw his bag over his shoulder

and headed for the door.

The minute he was gone, Willow spun around to face Jeanie. "You saw that flash, right?" she asked.

Jeanie nodded. She scanned the room again. "But nothing looks different."

Willow twirled her flower bracelet around. Her friend was right: Nothing looked different.

But something definitely *felt* different.

Magic crackled in the air like lightning. Willow could feel it prickling the back of her neck.

The World Genie Association handbook stated that every genie experienced the act of wish granting differently. Some heard bells. Some smelled strawberries. Some *literally* saw stars.

Willow's skin felt almost electric.

She *had* to have granted a wish. If she hadn't, she should probably go see the school nurse!

Jeanie looked at the clock and turned to her friend. "We should get to class."

The girls quickly packed up their things and headed to classroom 2B. Halfway there, Willow realized she'd left her library books back in the gym.

"I forgot something," she told Jeanie. "Can you wait a second?"

Jeanie sighed. "Okay, but hurry."

Willow sprinted back down the hall and burst into the gym.

The room was totally still. But that electric feeling prickled the back of her neck again.

It feels like a surprise party right before everyone jumps out and yells, "Surprise!" she thought.

"Hello?" Willow called.

No one answered.

Willow waited, but nothing happened. She shrugged, grabbed her books, and hurried from the gym.

Just before the doors closed behind her, a tiny sound stopped her in her tracks.

Was that a . . . horse's neigh? she wondered.

She shook her head. *No, it couldn't be. There's no one in the gym, and certainly not a horse!*

As she raced to meet Jeanie, Willow felt relieved that everything was fine. In fact, it was *better* than fine. It was library day *and* make-your-own-pizza night at Jeanie's house!

A FLOWER GROWS

"This last pepperoni ought to do it," Jeanie announced.

That evening the two friends were in the Bells' kitchen adding toppings to their pizzas. After spending the week looking at amazing art, Jeanie was feeling totally inspired. She'd arranged her pie toppings by color: green olives and peppers, yellow onions and pineapple, and red tomatoes and pepperoni.

"You deserve a prize for prettiest pizza," said Jeanie's mom.

"Definitely," said Willow. "But maybe not the tastiest. Pineapple? No thank you!"

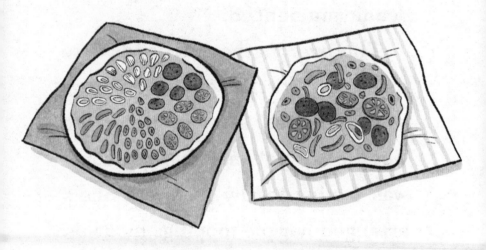

"I thought you liked creative ideas!" Jeanie teased.

Willow smiled as she reached for a piece of green pepper. "I do," she said. "But pizza is too important to—"

Willow stopped speaking.

Then Jeanie saw she was looking at a small yellow flower that had seemingly fluttered onto the table out of nowhere.

Jeanie's dad noticed it too. "Huh," he said. "I thought I swept around here after I closed the windows." Willow laughed nervously.

"You've got a little something behind your ear, dear," Jeanie's mom said, reaching over and pulling a long green tendril from Willow's hair.

Jeanie thought it looked like some kind of vine. At the end was a small pink flower!

"You must have gotten too close to the trellis outside!" Mr. Bell told Willow.

Willow nodded awkwardly and started twisting her bracelet.

Jeanie wondered: What was going on?

As Mr. Bell put their pizzas in the oven, Willow pulled on Jeanie's sleeve. "Um, could you help me fix my hair? In the bathroom?" she whispered.

Jeanie nodded and quickly followed Willow down the hall. When your best friend is a genie and she starts acting stranger than usual, something is definitely up.

Willow locked the door and turned to Jeanie. "I think that maybe the vine and flower came from my bracelet," Willow said.

That didn't make sense. "But you made your bracelet out of beads," Jeanie pointed out. "Not real flowers!"

"That's just it. I *did* make it out of beads," Willow said, thrusting her arm at Jeanie. The bracelet that had once been pretty, glittery beads was now slowly curling around her wrist.

Jeanie could barely believe her eyes. It was a real, live, *growing* plant.

Willow's bracelet—her art—had come to life!

Chapter 6

NOT-SO-STILL LIFE

Willow barely slept that night. She was too busy worrying about what her spell had unleashed. Leo had wished art would come alive . . . but she was pretty sure he didn't mean that *literally*.

The next day Willow rushed to get to school early. She and Jeanie had agreed to meet in the gym before class. Tonight was the art show's big opening, and they had to make sure the wish

hadn't messed up any of the projects.

Willow found her friend standing outside the gym, a funny look on her face.

Clop! Clop! Clop!

"Do you hear that?" Jeanie asked.

"It sounds like horse hooves!"

"I don't have a good feeling about this," Willow whispered.

"Me neither," said Jeanie. The two girls stepped toward the door. Together they opened it.

Oh no, thought Willow.

She could hardly believe her eyes!

Tigers from the animal and nature category were floating in the air. Leo's horse mobile whinnied and neighed as it galloped around the gym. Robots from the futuristic gallery had leaped off the canvases.

They raced and zoomed in a chorus of bleeps and bloops. A parade of papier-mâché musicians marched underneath the basketball hoops. And all of the botanical drawings were blooming right off the walls!

Willow glanced at Jeanie. Her friend's face was paler than a marble statue!

"What are we going to do?" Jeanie yelled over the noise.

Willow thought for a minute. Suddenly she had an idea.

Mr. Bloom always said that, with art, you can turn a mistake into something great. *And if not, use an eraser*, he'd joke.

"What if we try . . . erasing them?" Willow suggested.

Jeanie smiled. "Great idea!" she said.

The girls made a mad dash to the art room supply closet for as many erasers as they could find.

They returned to the gym, erasers in hand. Willow tried to catch her ballerina. But the dancer was too quick! She twirled out of Willow's grasp, leaving a couple of feathers behind.

Jeanie lunged for her picture of Bear. But just as she got close, the dots of paint flew apart . . . and put themselves back together over a basketball hoop.

Suddenly Jeanie heard a loud creak.

"The doors!" she shouted.

"Someone's coming!" cried Willow. "We can't let them see . . . any of this!"

Chapter 7

TINY TROUBLE . . . BIG PROBLEMS

Jeanie yanked the gym doors closed behind her and Willow.

"What gives?" asked Leo.

"We were just making sure all of the artwork seemed as . . . um . . . full of life . . . as we remembered," said Jeanie.

Leo grinned. "I can't wait to see!"

Jeanie's arms flew across the doors. "Oh, um, you don't want to go in there just yet," she said. "Because, um, we've been . . ."

"We're working on a surprise!" Willow interrupted. "It will be . . . performance art!"

"So cool! Can I get a sneak peek?" Leo asked.

"Sorry," said Willow. "The element of surprise is key to making this piece work."

Leo nodded. "I understand," he said. "And I respect your vision. I only wish the rest of our classmates took art as seriously as the two of you."

Jeanie let out a sigh of relief. It was a good thing Willow was great at thinking quickly!

Then Jeanie noticed Leo was holding a package under his arm. "What's that?" she asked.

"A new project," said Leo. "I was frustrated yesterday. But when I got home, inspiration struck!"

He unwrapped the package. To Jeanie, what Leo was holding looked like a regular, old mirror.

"I know this may look like a regular, old mirror," said Leo, "but the idea is that art reflects life *and* that art is what you make of it."

"Cool!" said Jeanie. "So the mirror is going to reflect all the artwork that's around it? And also that whatever we see in the mirror is what we want to see?"

"Exactly," said Leo.

"Okay, why don't we put your project inside for you?" Jeanie offered.

"Thanks!" Leo said, handing the mirror over to Jeanie. "See you in class!"

Back inside the gym the art show had turned into a circus. A lion and a rhino head-butted each other. The papier-mâché band played "Born to Be Wild." And a mob of manic pipe-cleaner people had climbed Leo's horse mobile and were riding the bucking bronco! It was total chaos!

"We don't have time to fix this right now," Jeanie told Willow as she set Leo's project in the corner. "The bell is about to ring. But the gym will be empty all day."

"We'll just have to sneak back here before tonight's grand opening," Willow added.

"At least the magic will all stay in one place!" Jeanie said as they grabbed their backpacks.

But just as they were about to leave, Jeanie realized she'd spoken too soon. A little purple pipe-cleaner cowboy ran out of the gym!

"Yee-haw!" he shouted as he sprinted down the hall.

"Oh no!" Jeanie cried.

Willow patted Jeanie's arm. "It'll be okay. After all, how much trouble can one little pipe cleaner get into?"

Jeanie wasn't sure . . . but she wasn't sure she wanted to find out.

Chapter 8

A GREAT ESCAPE GONE WRONG

The girls quickly walked into classroom 2B, dropped their bags in their cubbies, and slipped into their seats just before the morning bell rang.

"Good morning, everyone," began Ms. Patel. "Today we're going to continue our social studies unit on westward expansion. We'll start with a short film about the Oregon Trail."

Thank the stars! Willow thought as Ms. Patel dimmed the lights. She felt so zonked that she'd never have been able to focus on reading or join in one of her teacher's famous role-playing history lessons.

As the movie started, Willow tried to concentrate on the story of the settlers making their way across the plains in covered wagons.

But soon her mind started to wander. What was it like inside those wagons? Willow pictured a family traveling under a wide open sky. The father would drive the wagon, the mother beside him. Maybe the kids would sleep next to their dog, while outside the back of the wagon . . . a ballerina rode by on a horse!

I can't even get away from my magic in my daydreams, Willow thought, shaking the images out of her head.

She glanced at Jeanie, who was busily taking notes. Her friend was smart—Ms. Patel would probably quiz them on it later.

Willow went to grab a pencil from her desk. Just then she noticed something. She squinted. What was that? As she watched, a flash of purple climbed down the bookshelf and raced across the floor. It was the tiny pipe-cleaner person! He was scampering under Finn's desk and using a rubber band to . . . lasso a paper clip?

Willow's stomach clenched. She hadn't thought the pipe cleaner's escape was that big of a deal, but here he was in classroom 2B! That meant anyone could spot him. And if they did, they'd find out about Willow's spell. Then Willow would *never* become a master genie!

Willow thought fast. She'd have to pretend she dropped a pencil so she could sneak down onto the floor and catch the little purple dude.

But when she looked back down, the pipe-cleaner person was gone!

Chapter 9

OBJECTS IN MIRROR

"Do you think anyone else has seen him?" Jeanie whispered as she and Willow waited for everyone to leave classroom 2B.

It was lunchtime, but the girls planned to go back to the gym and try to clean up this magical mess before the art fair.

"I hope not," said Willow.

"Well, I'm just relieved no one

painted dragons," said Jeanie. "Can you imagine if . . ." She trailed off.

"Hey, is there a butterfly in here or something?" she could have sworn something had just flown by her nose.

"Um, I don't see anything," said Willow, scanning the room.

"There! Over there!" Jeanie cried.

It was the pipe-cleaner cowboy!
He was swinging on the string that
opened and closed the window
blinds.

"Yippee ki yay!" he cried as he leaped from the window.

The teensy cowboy gave them a small wave, bounded toward the door, and took off down the hall faster than a stampeding buffalo.

"Don't just stand there!" cried Jeanie. "We have to catch him!"

The girls rushed down the crowded hall, but the little purple figure was just too fast. He slid under sneakers, leaped up lockers, and danced over door frames. In a few seconds he was gone.

"Let's worry about the runaway later," said Jeanie when she'd caught her breath. "We have bigger problems to solve."

When they got to the gym, things were even wilder than before. The botanical drawings had grown up to the ceiling, the robots were going haywire, and the ballerina was spinning around and around in crazy circles... until she bumped into Leo's mirror. It wobbled back and forth... and back and forth.

As Jeanie and Willow stood there, terrified that the mirror was going to fall, Jeanie cried out, "Willow, isn't there *anything* in your genie manual about this?"

Willow suddenly gasped. "Yes!" she cried. "There's a part that says if you've accidentally brought something to life and it sees itself in a mirror, it gets scared and returns to its original state."

Before Jeanie could say a word, Willow ran over to the mirror and pointed it at the ballerina she'd worked so hard on. Then something strange happened. The ballerina got sucked right into the mirror and disappeared.

Willow started pointing the mirror at various art pieces around the room. As if the mirror were a giant vacuum, every piece of live art got sucked in.

When all the art had disappeared,
the room was quiet.

Willow looked nervous. Was the
art going to come back?

Suddenly each artwork shot back out of the mirror and into its rightful place as a still piece of art on a wall or pedestal, or wherever it had been before Willow's spell brought it to life.

When everything was back to normal, Jeanie let out a relieved sigh. "You did it!" she cried.

"*We did it*," said Willow.

That night the students and parents of classroom 2B gathered in the gym for the big opening.

As everyone admired the galleries, Mr. Bloom stepped in front of the crowd.

"Welcome, everyone, to the Rivertown Elementary School Art Fair! I'd like to—"

But before he could continue, a little purple figure tumbled across the floor . . . and hopped right onto Mr. Bloom's shoe! The pipe-cleaner cowboy raised a small triangle from the music room and opened the fair with a tiny *ting!*

For a long moment the gym was totally silent. Then Jeanie rushed forward and grabbed the cowboy while Willow faced the crowd.

"That's our project: Art in Action!" Willow announced.

All of the students and teachers and parents burst into applause.

Leo rushed over to the girls.

"That was some very amazing performance art!" he said. "You have to tell me how you did it!"

Jeanie smiled slyly. "A great magician—I mean a great *artist*—never reveals her secrets!"

Chapter 10

THE GENIE AND THE GENIUS

"Saturday afternoons are for sunshine, snacks, and staring at the clouds," said Willow.

Willow gazed dreamily at the cloudscape over the Bells' backyard, looking for ballerinas and robots and cowboys.

"Especially after a week like we had!" Jeanie added as she patted Bear's head.

Suddenly a small sparkling cloud appeared over Willow. The sound of wind chimes filled the air, and a tiny golden box floated down, right into Willow's hands.

"What is it?" asked Jeanie.

"Let's find out," Willow replied, lifting the lid. Inside Willow found a scroll and a badge embroidered with a painter's palette in golden thread. "It's from the World Genie Association!"

In recognition of your latest wish granting, we are pleased to award you the Enchanting Art badge. Congratulations on your achievement!

Sincerely,

The World Genie Association

"Willow, you did it!" Jeanie exclaimed, giving her friend a huge hug. "You're one step closer to becoming a Master Genie!"

Willow looked shocked. "I can't believe it!" she said. "I'm happy, but I know I need to learn to control my wish granting."

"Hey, at least you didn't grant a wish while we were on our field trip!" said Jeanie.

"That's true. I would *not* want to see the lions outside the library come to life," Willow joked. "Or Mr. Twister, that giant chocolate and vanilla mascot outside the Sweet Shoppe!" she stood and began twirling like a giant soft-serve ice cream swirl.

"I've got brain freeze just thinking about it!" Jeanie laughed.

"The truth is, I never could have earned this badge without you," Willow said. "You may not be a genie, but you're a *genius*."